The Dragonfly Kite

First published in 2009
by Wayland

Text copyright © Liss Norton 2009
Illustration copyright © Emma McCann 2009

Wayland
338 Euston Road
London NW1 3BH

Wayland Australia
Hachette Children's Books
Level 17/207 Kent Street
Sydney, NSW 2000

Series Editor: Louise John
Editor: Katie Powell
Cover design: Paul Cherrill
Design: D.R.ink
Consultant: Shirley Bickler

A CIP catalogue record for this book is available from the British Library.

ISBN 9781526302656

Printed in China

Wayland is a division of Hachette Children's Books,
an Hachette UK Company

www.hachette.co.uk

The Dragonfly Kite

Written by Liss Norton
Illustrated by Emma McCann

WAYLAND

Fergus the Superfrog was playing
ball with his best friend, Doris,
when he heard someone sobbing.

"Doris, can you hear that noise?"
asked Fergus. "It sounds like
someone's very upset."

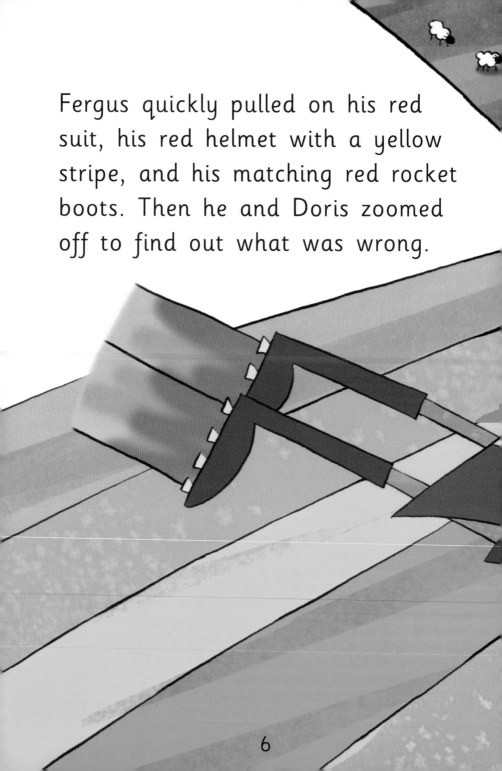

Fergus quickly pulled on his red suit, his red helmet with a yellow stripe, and his matching red rocket boots. Then he and Doris zoomed off to find out what was wrong.

Fergus and Doris flew past the local school. They could see lots of children playing hula hoop in the school playground, but no one looked upset.

"Fergus, over there!" said Doris, and
she pointed to a girl sitting on a
bench all by herself.

Fergus flew over and sat down beside her.
"What's wrong?" he asked.

"Everyone wants to play hula hoop, but I can't do it," the girl sobbed.

"Don't cry," Doris said. "Fergus will help. He's a Superfrog. What's your name?"

"Grace," replied the girl. "Will you really be able to help me?"
Grace looked hopefully at Fergus.

Fergus thought for a moment.
"I know just what to do," he said.
"Can you get me some paper and
a ball of string?"

Grace ran into school and came
back with the things Fergus needed.

"Doris, can you find me two sticks, please?" Fergus asked.

So, Doris sped off to look for the sticks.

Fergus showed Grace how to tear and fold the paper.

Doris soon returned with the sticks.
Fergus stuck the paper to them in a
cross. Then Grace tied the paper
to them.

"What are you making?"
asked Doris.

"You'll see," grinned Fergus, as he tied the string to one of the sticks.

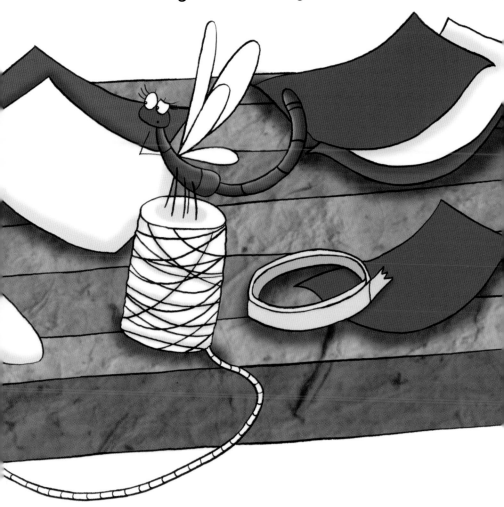

"There," he said at last. "All done!"

"It's a kite!" Grace said.
"And it looks just like me!"
exclaimed Doris.

They had made a beautiful
dragonfly kite with a purple and
blue body and big white wings.

"While everyone is hula hooping, you can play with your kite," Fergus said.

Grace looked up at the bright
blue sky.

"It doesn't look very windy.
Do you think it will fly?"

"Definitely," cried Fergus, and using all of his Superfrog powers, Fergus started to blow very hard.

Suddenly, the kite soared
out of Grace's hands, high
up into the air.
"It's flying!" she cried.

The other children stopped playing
with their hoops and watched
the kite.

"Look at it go!" said Ben. "Can I play, Grace?"

"Me, too!" cried Lucy.

Fergus got to work folding
and tearing more paper at
Superfrog speed.

Grace helped him, while Doris flew
off to find more sticks. Soon
everyone had a kite.

Fergus took another deep breath.
Using his Superfrog powers again,
he blew all the kites into the air.

"This is much better than
hula hooping," said Ben.
"Hooray for Superfrog!"

"Thanks, Fergus," said Grace. "You're the best!"

START READING is a series of highly enjoyable books for beginner readers. **The books have been carefully graded to match the Book Bands widely used in schools.** This enables readers to be sure they choose books that match their own reading ability.

Look out for the Band colour on the book in our Start Reading logo.

The Bands are:

	Pink Band 1A & 1B
	Red Band 2
	Yellow Band 3
	Blue Band 4
	Green Band 5
	Orange Band 6
	Turquoise Band 7
	Purple Band 8
	Gold Band 9

START READING books can be read independently or shared with an adult. They promote the enjoyment of reading through satisfying stories supported by fun illustrations.

Liss Norton used to be a teacher. She now writes books, musicals and plays for children. She is keen on growing organic fruit and veg at her allotment, on her granddaughters, Maddie and Arabella, and on visiting castles. One day she hopes to find a secret passage...

Emma McCann is currently living a dual life. By day, she is a mild-mannered illustrator, but by night she becomes the masked crime-fighter and master cake-baker "Red Velvet". She hopes to be joined soon in her crime fighting/cake baking adventures by a small, dog-shaped partner.